猴
Monkey

羊
Sheep

馬
Horse

狗
Dog

蛇
Snake

豬
Pig

龍
Dragon

鼠
Rat

兔
Rabbit

牛
Ox

虎
Tiger

For nearly 5,000 years, the Chinese culture
has organized time in cycles of twelve years.
This Eastern calendar is based upon the movement
of the moon (as compared to the Western which
follows the sun), and is symbolized by the zodiac circle.
An animal that has unique qualities represents each
year. Therefore, if you are born in a particular year,
then you share the personality of that animal. Now
people worldwide celebrate this two-week-long
festival in the early spring and enjoy the
start of another Chinese New Year.

To my mother, Naida, the queen of our house.
—O.C.

For my mother, who has always supported and encouraged me to pursue my dreams.
—K.O.

immedium

Immedium, Inc.
P.O. Box 31846
San Francisco, CA 94131
www.immedium.com

Text Copyright © 2016 Oliver Chin
Illustrations Copyright © 2016 Kenji Ono

For information about special discounts for bulk purchases, please contact Immedium Special Sales at sales@immedium.com.

First hardcover edition published 2016.

Edited by Don Menn
Book design by Erica Loh Jones
Chinese translation by Hsiaoying Chen

Printed in Malaysia
10 9 8 7 6 5 4 3 2 1

Library of Congress Cataloging-in-Publication Data

Chin, Oliver Clyde, 1969-
  The year of the monkey : tales from the Chinese zodiac / by Oliver Chin ; illustrated by Kenji Ono. -- First hardcover edition.
      pages cm. -- (Tales from the Chinese zodiac ; 11)
  Summary:"The monkey Max befriends the boy Kai, as well as other animals of the Chinese lunar calendar, and demonstrates the qualities of an adventurous spirit. Lists the birth years and characteristics of individuals born in the Chinese Year of the Monkey"-- Provided by publisher.
  ISBN 978-1-59702-118-0 (hardback) -- ISBN 1-59702-118-0 (hardcover)
  [1. Monkeys--Fiction. 2. Astrology, Chinese--Fiction. 3. Animals--Fiction.] I. Ono, Kenji, 1975- illustrator. II. Title.
  PZ7.C44235Ydq 2016
  [E]--dc23
                        2015012879

ISBN: 978-1-59702-118-0

The Year of the Monkey

Tales from the Chinese Zodiac

十二生肖故事系列 猴年的故事

Written by Oliver Chin
Illustrated by Kenji Ono

文： 陈曜豪
图： 大野贤二

immedium
www.immedium.com
San Francisco. CA

The Monkey King was a legendary prankster who performed miraculous feats. He carried a magic staff and flew on the clouds.

美猴王孙悟空是个著名的捣蛋鬼，他能变出很多令人惊奇的把戏。 他随身带着一根金箍棒，还能驾着觔斗云腾云驾雾。

Luckily he found a lovely Queen. They settled down and had a baby named Max.

美猴王很幸运地遇到了他的皇后，他们一起生活，然后有了孩子，他们叫他麦思。

The Jade Emperor was a wise ruler, with a staff of scholars, soldiers, and secretaries. Smiling upon the infant, he proclaimed, "If this child follows in his parents' footsteps, heaven below had better take notice."

玉皇大帝是一位有智慧的统治者，他统领着一群学者、士兵和大臣。他微笑地看着小猴子，说："如果小猴子个性像他爸爸的话，凡间的人可就要小心喽。"

Sure enough, Max was quite a handful. "He's a chimp off the old block," marveled the Queen.

果然不出玉皇大帝所料，麦思是只不受控制的小猴子。"他的个性和他爸爸简直一模一样，"猴后惊奇地说。

Energetic and curious, the little monkey climbed mountains, swung through forests, and leapt over rivers.

小猴子总是充满着活力和好奇心，他爬过山峦，他穿过森林，他跃过溪流。

Out on the town he couldn't sit down, even when eating! A mischievous tot, Max declared, **"I want to learn all the family tricks!"**

His father replied, "Well, we certainly have a lot of them!"

在外面的时候他总是不能安静地坐下来，甚至连吃饭的时候也不行！淘气的麦思宣布："我想要学会所有家传的把戏！"

他的爸爸回答："家传的把戏可多着呢！"

Before long Max started school. On the first day, his teacher told the students, "Behave and pay attention." But listening quietly and following orders was hard for restless kids to do, especially Max.

不久之后，麦思上了学。 在开学的第一天，老师告诉所有的学生："大家要守规矩，上课要专心。"但是对于静不下来的小朋友来说，这是一件很困难的事，尤其是麦思。

He daydreamed of doing heroic deeds. **"Oo-oo, Aa-aa!"** he yelled. Yet he realized that he was still in class!

他做着白日梦，幻想自己做着英勇的事迹。"呜，啊！"他大声叫。 但他马上意识到自己还在班上上课。

Max had to clean up the room and visit the principal's office, which did not please his parents.

他被罚了清理教室，还得去见校长，他的父母很不高兴。

However, at recess and lunch, Max was free to express himself on the playground. There he scaled the jungle gym, skipped across the monkey bars, and swung high with his new friends such as Kai.

在课间活动和午饭时间，麦思才能随心所欲地做他想做的事。 从攀爬架最底端往上爬，一直爬到最高点，从单杠的一头越过另一头，再和他的新朋友们一起荡秋千，在上头越荡越高，小凯就是他的新朋友之一。

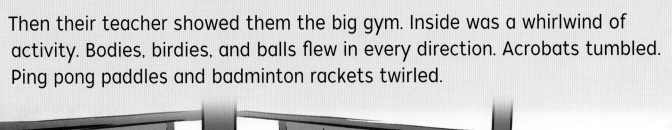

Then their teacher showed them the big gym. Inside was a whirlwind of activity. Bodies, birdies, and balls flew in every direction. Acrobats tumbled. Ping pong paddles and badminton rackets twirled.

接下来的时间，老师领着他们来到了一个诺大的体育馆。体育馆里到处都是人，他们正在进行着各式各样的活动。从每一个方向都看得到有人忙着传接羽毛球或其他球类。还有人在地上翻滚，姿势像是耍杂技的。大家手上的乒乓球拍和羽球拍，不停地转动。

"Max, come here!" exclaimed Kai. "You'll get a kick out of this."
This sport seemed like the others, where one had to knock
an object over a net to someone on the other side.

"What's the big deal?" replied Max.

"麦思，你过来!"小凯兴奋
地叫。"你会喜欢这个的。"
这项运动跟某些运动很像，
需要把一样东西传给站在
网子另一方的人。

"这有什么了不起的？"
麦思回答。

But here both players kicked a feathered weight. No hands allowed! Legs shot higher and feet flicked faster than Max thought possible.

但进行这项活动的时候，两个人都要用脚踢一个系上羽毛的小重物。 你不能用手碰它! 麦思没想到玩这种游戏时，腿要抬这么高，脚要踢这么快。

The Coach explained, "This sport is called 'Jianzi' or shuttlecock."

教练解释："这个叫做毽子。"

Meanwhile a crowd gathered around center court. "Make way for the Dragon and Tiger," boasted their trainer the General. The serpent did the "Dragon Tail" exercise. The big cat did the "Sitting Tiger."

这时候，人们开始往体育馆的中心聚集。"让个地方给龙和老虎吧，"他们的训练员将军神气地说。龙表演了"龙尾"，而老虎表演了"坐虎"。

Coach gushed, "They are the best team in the land." So the kids tried copying them. Serving, returning, and volleying were harder than they looked! But Max liked the challenge of learning the new game.

教练激动地说："他们是世界上最棒的选手。"所有的小朋友都想像他们一样。发毽子、回传毽子和长射毽子可不像看起来那么简单。但是麦思喜欢学习新的游戏，接受新的挑战，所以他不害怕。

Max and Kai had fun and returned to play regularly. Finishing a rally, Max hollered, **"Oo-oo, Aa-aa!"**

麦思和小凯玩得很开心，他们常常回去踢毽子。 在踢了一场毽子之后，麦思大叫："呜，啊！"

"You have talent," observed the Coach. "Practice your technique and not your talking, and you'll go far."

"你很有天分，"教练观察麦思的表现后说道。"好好地练习，不要爱说话，你会很有成绩的。"

Inspired, Max started kicking the shuttlecock at home. **"Right, left. Right, left."**

His father asked, "What are you doing?"

受到教练的鼓励之后，麦思开始在家里练习踢毽子。"左、右、左、右。"

他的父亲问："你在做什么呀？"

Max answered, **"I'm going to be the best jianzi player."** But his mother frowned and shook her head.

麦思回答："我要成为一个最会踢毽子的人。"但是他的母亲皱了皱眉，摇了摇头。

"Honey, don't play silly games," advised the Monkey Queen. "You can accomplish extraordinary things, just like us." Then she regaled Max with some of their famous adventures.

"亲爱的，别再玩那个可笑的游戏了，"猴后劝告麦思。"你能够成就不平凡的大事，就像我们一样。"接着她告诉了麦思一些他们经历过的著名冒险故事。

Hearing these amazing stories, Max doubted whether his hobby was worth it. Watching his buddies, he wondered if his fate lay elsewhere, to succeed at grand challenges that no one else dare try.

听完了这些故事之后，麦思开始思考他的新嗜好到底有没有意义。 看着自己的好朋友们，他想着他是不是命中注定要做一些别的事情，他是不是该挑战一些没有人敢尝试的事情。

That weekend Max's family saw a poster for the annual shuttlecock tournament. The chef crowed, "The champions are unbeatable!"

The waiter barked, "The Flying Dragon Kick is unstoppable!"

那个周末，麦思的家人看到了一张年度踢毽子比赛的海报。厨师欢叫："没有人能打败那个冠军队！"

侍应生大声喊叫："飞龙的脚上功夫是没有人能比得上的！"

Face The Great Wall at the Jianzi Open

Buy your tickets today!

The monk predicted, "It would take a miracle for anyone else to win."

"Those odds look good to me," winked the Monkey King, who nudged his son.

Max took a second look and muttered, **"Maybe you're right."**

和尚预测:"除非有奇迹,否则没有人能赢得了他们的。"

"看起来你很有機會哦。"美猴王轻推一下他的儿子,眨了眨眼睛说。

麦思转头又看了一眼海报,自言自语地说:"或许你是对的。"

The next day Max asked Kai, **"Do you want to enter the jianzi tournament?"**
The partners smiled, shook hands, and went to the gym.

第二天，麦思问了小凯："你想参加踢毽子
比赛吗？"他们对着对方发出会心一笑，
握了握手，两位搭档一起走向了体育馆。

The Coach told them, "You two need to join the team first."

教练告诉他们："你们两个得先加入毽子队。"

So the pair practiced diligently. They did the "Leopard Head" and "Standing Crane."

他们两个非常认真地练习。 他们练了几个踢毽子的招式，像是"豹头"和"鹤立"。

Letting his actions speak for himself, Max bounced the birdie wherever he went and improved with each step.

麦思的行动证明了一切，不管走到哪里，他总是在练习踢毽子，他一点一点地进步。

Max and Kai became the school's best doubles squad, then rose through the county's ranks. At the tournament tryouts, they tackled older teams and barely qualified! Now the big match was a week away.

麦思和小凯成为学校最佳的双人组合,他们在地区的排名也提升了很多。 在预赛的时候,他们对上了许多经验老道的队伍,差一点就不能晋级了。 眼看离最重要的比赛,就只剩下一个星期的时间。

At home Max wondered,
"How can I get better?"

Impressed by his devotion, Mom suggested, "A champ needs a special move."

回到家后，
麦思思考着："我要怎样才能踢得更好呢？"

麦思的努力打动了他的母亲，她建议麦思：
"猴子们应该用猴子专属的招式。"

Dad replied, "I have a trick up my sleeve." Together they drilled until Max got it right.

他的爸爸回答："我有个独门绝招能够传授给你。"

他们一起练习，一直到麦思能正确地踢出这个招式。

Finally the contest began! The town swelled with fans and festivities. At the arena, Max and Kai's classmates cheered them on. The confident rookies cruised past the first round and survived the second.

比赛终于开始了！小镇上到处是毽子迷，还有各式各样的庆祝活动。 麦思和小凯的同学在运动场上为他们加油、欢呼。 这两个充满自信的伙伴轻易地拿下了第一轮，接着也在第二轮比赛获得胜利。

In their semifinal, they confronted the Snake, a slick passer and kicker. But with Max's speed and range, the duo squeaked into the finals.

在半决赛的时候，他们对上了蛇。 蛇传毽子和踢毽子的动作十分灵巧，但是相比之下，麦思的速度和变化更胜一筹，他们因此险胜而进入了决赛。

Everyone was very surprised! "That's our boy!" shouted Max's parents.

大家都好惊讶!"他是我们的儿子!"麦思的父母大声地喊道。

Now they faced the Tiger and Dragon. These bruisers had bowled through their bracket, barely breaking a sweat. They looked down on their challengers. The General huffed, "Get ready to be runners-up."

现在他们对上了老虎和龙。 这两个壮汉轻轻松松就晋级了，并没有花费他们一点力气。 他们根本看不起他们的对手。 将军轻蔑地喊道："你们准备拿第二名吧。"

这两个强悍的野兽赢得了第一局的胜利。但在第二局比赛的时候，两位小将用尽全力，放手一搏。他们抓住机会，夺回失去的分数，战成了平手。第三局将是决定胜负的一战。

The big beasts roared ahead
to win the first set. But in the second, the youngsters hung on
tooth and nail. Snatching an opening, they clawed their way back to even the score.
The third set was the tiebreaker!

Back and forth they battled.
Then the kids scratched
out a slim lead and earned
a match point. Max took a
deep breath...and served a rocket!
Dragon slashed a ferocious return.

他们来回地交战，然后小将们取得了些许的优势，得到了追平的一分。 麦思深深地吸了一口气，再以火箭般的速度将毽子发给对手！龙猛然地回传。

Next Kai made a lunging save.

接着小凯飞扑过来，把毽子接起。

However, Tiger hit a towering lob. The birdie zoomed beyond their reach toward the corner. Yet Max leapt high, like he was climbing a rainbow.

His tail spinning in a blur, Max cried, **"Oo-oo, Aa-aa!"**

然而，老虎却踢高了毽子。 毽子迅速地飞向大家触碰不到的角落。 这时麦思一跃而上，像是要攀上彩虹那样。

他抬起尾巴，在模糊中快速旋转，麦思大叫：
"呜！啊！"

The fireball smashed through the Tiger and Dragon's defense and crashed inside the line. Max's "Monkey Spike" won the game!

In disbelief, the Coach announced, "Wow! The crowd has gone bananas!"

毽子像是火球一般击破了老虎和龙的防线,在界线内坠落了下来。 麦思的"猴子强力扣杀"让他们赢得了比赛!

教练不敢相信地说:"群众们要发狂了!"

Awarding the victors their trophy, the Jade Emperor remarked, "This upset shows us that magic can still surprise us all." Delighted, the Monkey King and Queen hugged their little prince.

把奖杯颁发给胜利者之后，玉皇大帝说："你们意外的胜利，让大家对你们出神入化的表现感到惊喜。"美猴王和他的皇后高兴地抱着他们的小王子。

Max and Kai continued to be fun-loving pals. Like most kids, they enjoyed going to school and learning their lessons.

麦思和小凯依旧是一对爱玩的伙伴。 像其他的孩子一样，他们喜欢去学校，也喜欢学习新知识。

Meanwhile, they managed to conduct their fair share of monkey business.

在这同时，他们还是能兼顾他们喜欢做的"猴子事业"。

Always finding his own way, Max savored the sweet things in life like a ripe peach. And everyone agreed that it was an incredible Year of the Monkey.

麦思总是能找到享受美好人生的方式，像是品尝甜美熟透的桃子一样。 大家都觉得，这一年是美好的猴年。

猴

Monkey 生肖猴

1920, 1932, 1944, 1956, 1968, 1980, 1992, 2004, 2016, 2028

People born in the Year of the Monkey are carefree, curious, and crafty. They are playful, nimble, and persistent. But they can be impetuous and naughty, and sometimes show off. Though they are fond of mischief, monkeys keep their eyes on the prize and are indispensable allies.

在猴年出生的人是无忧无虑、充满好奇心而且聪明狡猾的。 他们有爱玩、聪明机智、能坚持到底的个性。 但有些时候，他们会比较没有耐性、调皮，也会比较爱现。 虽然大家觉得他们很淘气，但猴子们对自己所设定的目标总是勇往直前，也是大家不可缺少的伙伴。